D0417101

C0000 002 624 469

Dedicated to Dora Bloom
- DP

For Grace Halligan
with much love
- SC

First published in 2012
by Scholastic Children's Books
Euston House, 24 Eversholt Street
London NW1 1DB
a division of Scholastic Ltd
www.scholastic.co.uk
London ~ New York ~ Toronto ~ Sydney ~ Auckland
Mexico City ~ New Delhi ~ Hong Kong

Text copyright © 2012 Daniel Postgate
Illustrations copyright © 2012 Sam Childs

PB ISBN 978 1407 115 39 9

All rights reserved
Printed in Singapore

1 3 5 7 9 10 8 6 4 2

The moral rights of Daniel Postgate and Sam Childs have been asserted.

Papers used by Scholastic Children's Books are made from wood
grown in sustainable forests.

Friends
in the
Snow

Daniel Postgate & Sam Childs

■ SCHOLASTIC

When Lucy's dad painted her bedroom wall,
he painted it a nice bright

white.

"What shall we have on it?"
Dad asked Lucy. "Some flowers?
A rainbow? Butterflies?"

"White is nice," said Lucy.
"Just **white**?" said Dad.

"It's not **just** white," Lucy laughed.

"It's a **white monster**
in the **white snow!**"

Lucy wished she hadn't said anything about a monster.

That night the monster kept her awake with his grunting and howling.

"Please go away," said Lucy.
"I can't," sighed the monster.
"There's nowhere to go...
There's nothing but **white**."

"I'm sure there must be **something**,"
said Lucy, and she led him off into the
   white,
     white,
      white to find out.

But the monster was quite right – there was nothing but **white**.

"What would you like to see?"
Lucy asked.

"A friend," said the monster.
"A friend would be nice."

"A penguin?" suggested Lucy.
"I'm not choosey," said the monster.

"A penguin it is then." said Lucy. "Let's make it a king penguin!"

And just about then they saw something far away in the white.

"Off we go!" called Lucy.

And off they went.

That something grew nearer...

and nearer...

and nearer...and nearer...

until finally they could see what it was.

A fabulous castle with a penguin on top!

"Hello, my new friend!"
grinned the monster.

There was a long silence before
the penguin finally spoke.

"I'm not your friend," he said.
"I'm far too important to have friends.
I am king after all... and this is my kingdom."

"But what are you king of?" asked Lucy.
"There's nothing here but white, white, white."

The penguin looked north, south, east and west.

He saw that Lucy was quite right,
there was nothing but white.

"Then I'm King of Nothing,"
said the penguin. "And Nothing
will have to do."

"I think you had better wish for something else," Lucy whispered in the monster's ear, "and forget about silly penguins."

The monster looked at the penguin.
He seemed very proud, but very sad.
The monster made a wish...

...And just about then a rocket appeared in the white.

"That's a strange present to wish for," said Lucy.
"Watch," said the monster.

WHOOSH! went the rocket.

And a thousand, thousand stars sprinkled
down onto the white. Where they landed,
a tree or a bush or a stream or a rock
fizzled and popped into life.

"It's a kingdom! A kingdom for me! Oh, thank you!"
cried the delighted penguin, and he danced about
on top of his castle.

"Now I must give you a present," the penguin told the monster. "Please have my crown," he said, "and you can be king."

"Oh no, no, no," said the monster, "I don't want to be king."

"But...I have nothing else to give you," said the penguin, looking at his crown.

"Yes you have!" said the monster. "You have your friendship –
you could be my friend!"

The penguin laughed. "You're such a kind monster," he said,
"I'd like to think I already am your friend."

Then, paw in flipper, they went
off to explore their new kingdom.

"Goodbye!" they said to Lucy.

"Goodbye," murmured Lucy.

But they couldn't hear her. They were already gone, and Lucy was fast asleep.

The next morning Lucy asked her dad
if he could paint her white wall **blue**.

"Just **blue**?" asked her dad.
"It won't be **just** blue…" laughed Lucy.

The End